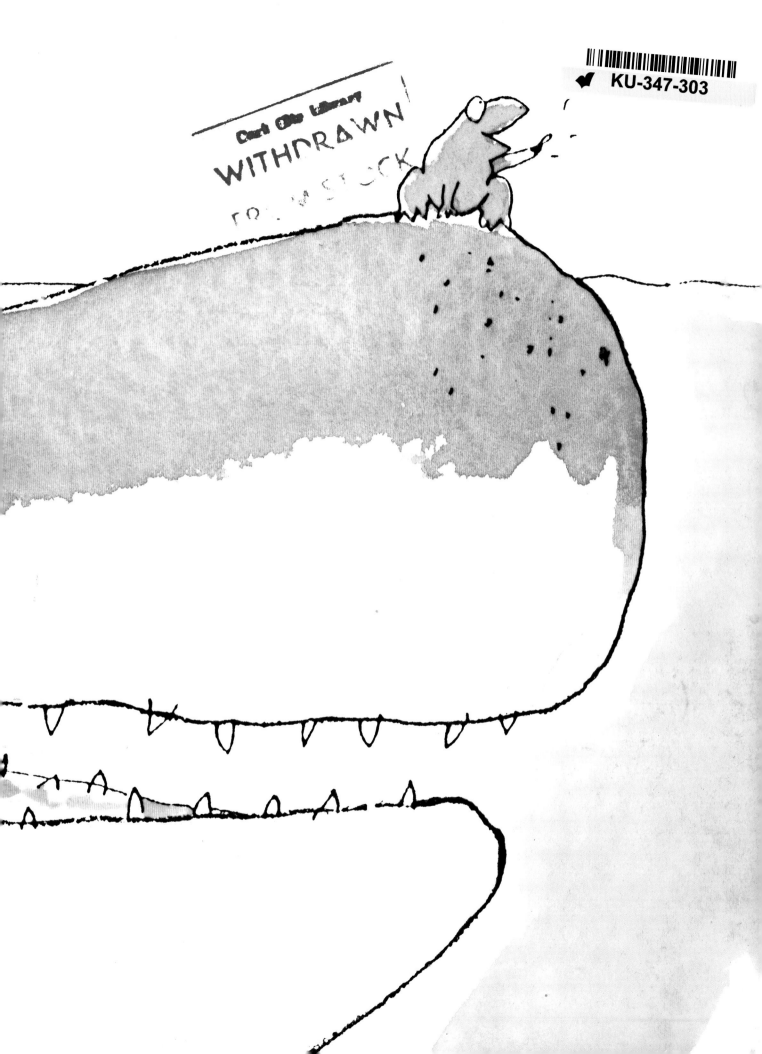

For Mum and Dad
T. W.

First published in Great Britain in 2004
by Boxer Books Limited
www.boxerbooks.com

Text and illustrations copyright © 2004 Tom Willans

ISBN 0-9547373-0-X

Printed in China

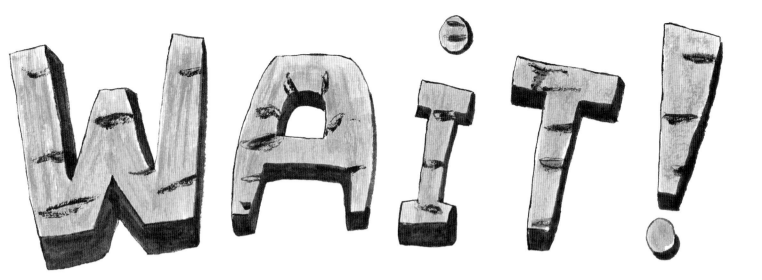

WAIT!

I want to tell you a story!

Tom Willans

Boxer Books

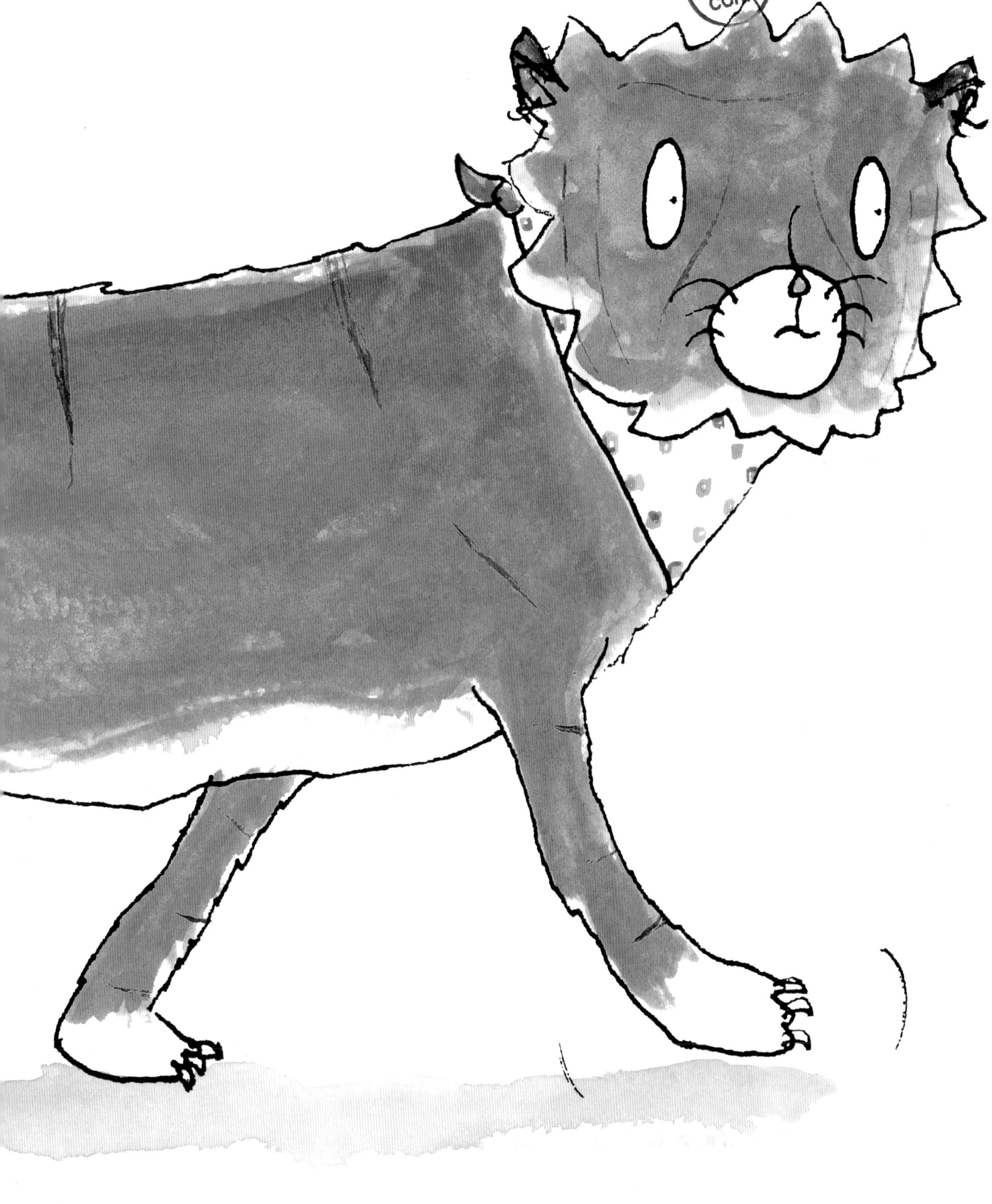

Once there was a muskrat sitting quietly by a tree.

Along came a tiger.

"I'm going to eat you little muskrat."
Said the tiger.

"Wait!"

Said the muskrat.
"I want to tell you a story."

"Okay," said the tiger,
"But make it quick!"

"Once upon a time,"
said the muskrat,
"there was a frog sitting on a pond.
A big shark came up through the
water and said, I'm going to eat you
little frog."

"Wait!"

Said the frog.
"I want to tell you a story."
"Okay," said the shark,
"but make it quick!"

"Once upon a time,"
said the frog,
"there was a lizard
sitting on a rock.
A big snake came along
and said, I'm going
to eat you little lizard."

"Wait!"

Said the lizard.
"I want to tell you a story."

"Okay," said the snake,
"but make it quick!"

"Once upon a time," said the lizard,
"there was a fly sitting on a web.
A big spider came along and said,
I'm going to eat you little fly."

"Wait!"

said the fly,
"I want to tell you a story."
"I don't want to hear it!"
said the spider.
And ate the fly.

" And I," said the tiger,
"am going to eat you little muskrat!"

"Wait!"

Shouted the muskrat.
"There's more..."

... "the lizard ate the spider,

the snake ate the lizard,

the frog ate the snake,

and the shark ate the frog."

"What happened then?"
Asked the tiger.

"The crocodile ate the tiger."
Said the muskrat.

"What crocodile?"

Asked the Tiger.

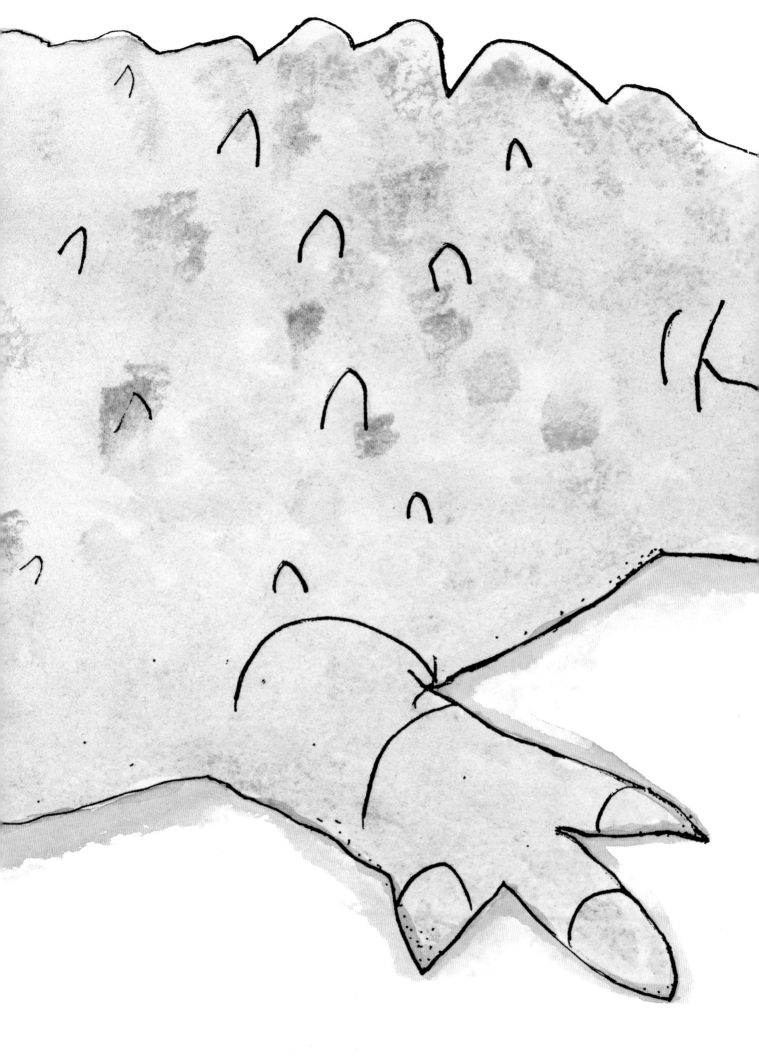

And the muskrat got away.